HAPPENSTANCE

THE JOURNEY THAT SHOULD NOT HAVE HAPPENED

Written and Illustrated by

ESTELA T DOMAOAL

Happenstance
Estela T Domaoal

www.whitefalconpublishing.com

First Edition, 2023

ISBN - 979-8-89222-091-0

To the lovers of heavenly bodies, may this book inspire you to explore space in your ways.

"It is a paradox to live in two worlds, standing on the horizon where dreams become a reality."

The plan to navigate planet Mars was on. For several years, four astronauts had prepared for the journey the world had eagerly waited for. The training was secretive and sensitive, only known to a handful.

Launch day had arrived. Astronauts A and C occupied the driving seats. However, there was no sign of Astronauts B and D, and Spaceship Azure took off in five minutes. Nothing could stop it.

Two robots, One and Two, came out of one door, looking dejected. They failed the written land navigation test thrice and now consoled each other. Out of the adjacent door, Master Orange stepped out, feeling sore.

Confounded that the team of four astronauts was incomplete, Master Orange grabbed the two robots, dressed them in space suits, and commanded them to march into the spaceship. No one knew that two astronauts and two robots were the Master's crew.

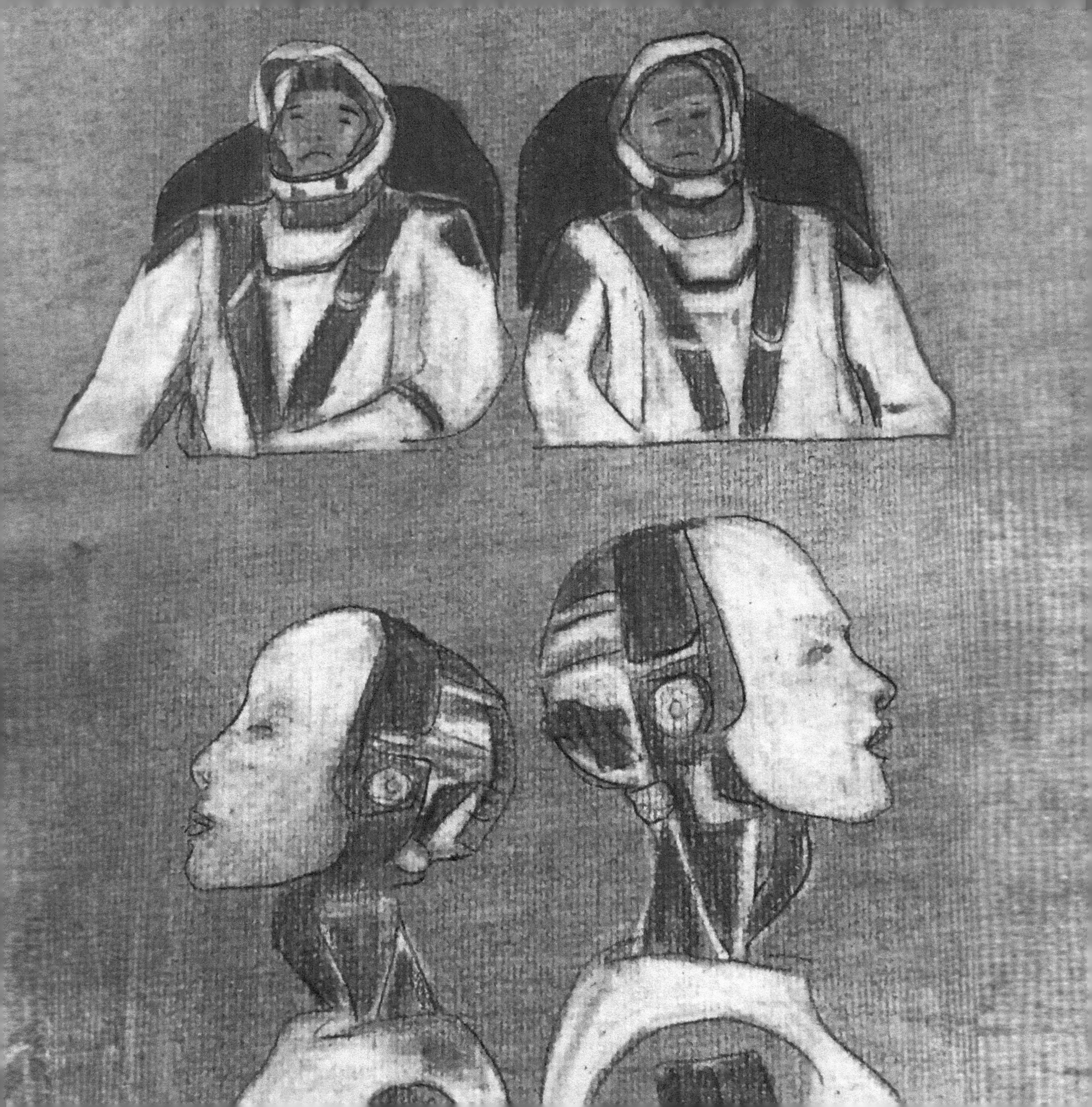

Speechless Astronauts A and C welcomed the new teammates hesitantly. There was no time to process the dramatic change of plan.

5,4,3,2,1 the rocket flew!

As the rocket soared, Master Orange realized his impulsive decision to take the robots as crew members was a mistake. A big mistake, indeed!

A team of two pairs commanded Azure. While one pair operated the ship, the other would rest to eat, sleep or recover.

In one instance, the robots were in charge while the two men were asleep. The connection between the ship and the Earth controller stopped without any warning. It did not concern Robots One and Two.

They took out of a locker a printed map that functioned as the backup navigator and continued with the job. They had failed some navigation tests, but they were smart enough to know where to find the contingency plan - the savior in times of crisis.

The team traveled and passed thousands of stars, rocks and unidentified objects for a long time. They were awed, amazed and petrified.

As soon as they descended back to their homeland, endless stories from the four overflowed.

They shared all the photographs, collected objects and recorded information with their fellow astronauts and robots on Earth.

Exploding with glee, the boss arrived. “How was Mars?” he asked.

“Far different from what we all thought.”

“Not hot at all.”

“All covered with ice.”

“We felt so light out there.”

A roar of laughter enveloped the room. As the boss pointed out the calendar, the team realized they had been away for ten years. Everyone knew that a trip to Mars took up to three years. A blunder of time?

Scratching their heads with mixed bewilderment, the boss came to the rescue.

“Far different from everyone’s expectations? Hmm, let me put it this way.

You did not reach Mars.

The disconnection from here should have taken a few hours to fix. But when your ship detoured, we did not reconnect and thought we’d lost you.

Years of perseverance paid off, though. We conquered our fears, worked ourselves into a sweat and gathered the strength to get you back. The reconnection between us was our most significant victory here.

My dear folks, you sat foot on Europa, one of Jupiter’s major moons. With luck, we gained a far greater prize.

Although it was not the mission we aimed for, it is the task of the next generation.

Gosh, we all did it!”

Robots One and Two looked at each other and confessed how they snatched some navigation maps when the controller's connection broke without giving it much thought.

"Sorry about the big mess, boss. Also, when you approached us to join the dream team, we wanted to tell you how incapable we were because we f_ _f failed the navigation tests," came the sheepish voice.

"Nonsense!

Failing the theory test was likely to happen. Being out in space, surviving and trusting yourself was the test of skill and bravery. One door closes and another opens.

The maps may have been a big mistake, but we made the impossible possible. A chance discovery. Well done to everybody in this room!"

Cheers, jeers and teasing continued until someone emptied the last wine bottle.

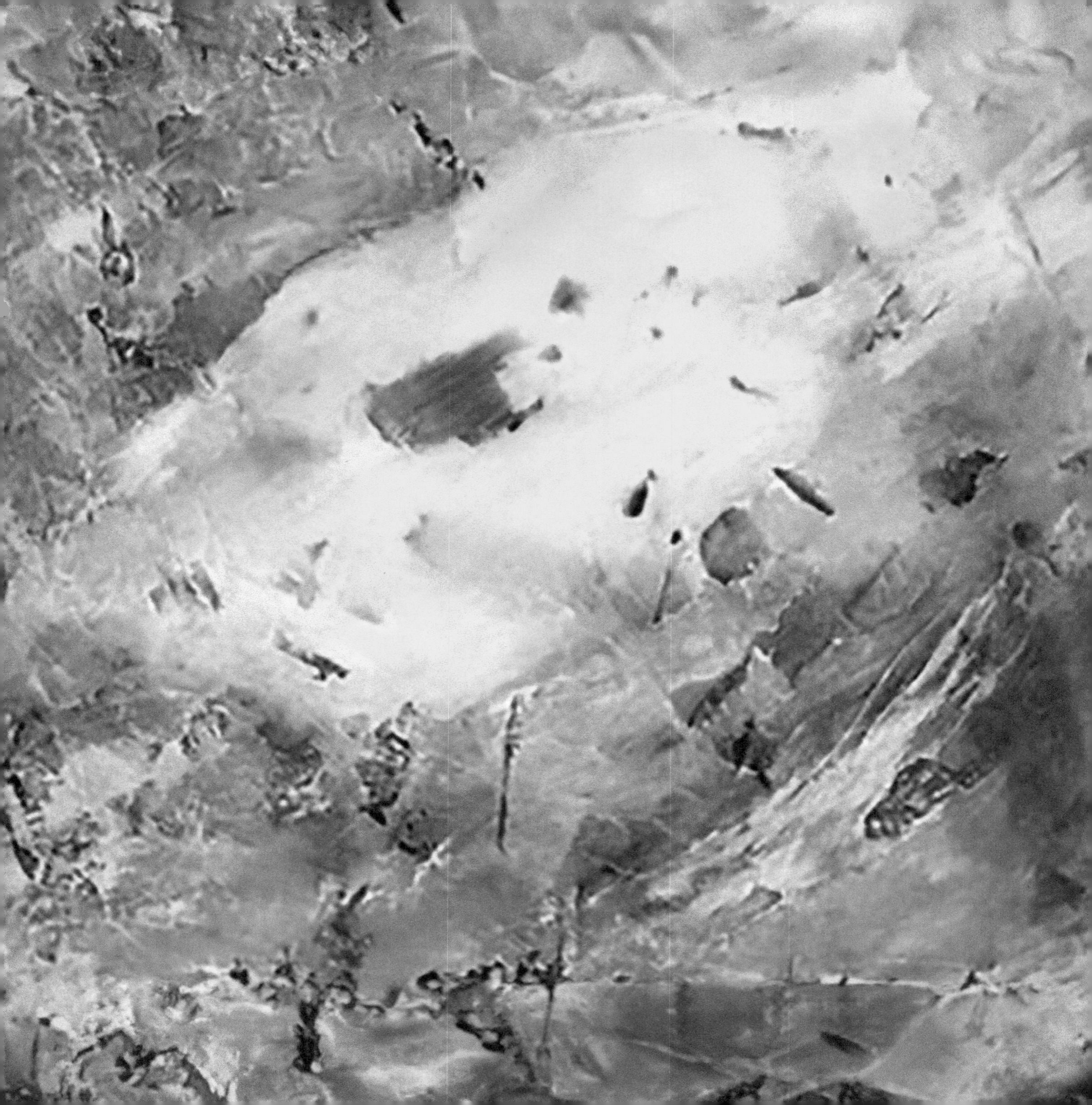

'I can't stop!'

'Go, Nelson!' his friend Abra shouted. Nelson didn't look at the boys but there was a light in his eyes.

Nelson **ran**. His feet moved quickly on the road. One, two, one, two ... he ran for three **kilometres**, four, five. He was in the sun but he wasn't **tired**. He loved running. It was his **life**. The road **felt** good under his feet.

Old Jacob Mutwa was at his door. 'Where are you running today, Nelson?'

'River Street. A letter for Miss Tlali from her sister.'

'You're a good boy!' The old man smiled. 'Can you take a letter for *me* tomorrow?'

ran /ræn/ (v, past tense of **run**) I never walked to school. I always *ran*.
kilometre /ˈkɪləmiːtəʳ/ (n) My school is a *kilometre* from my house.
tired /taɪəd/ (adj) I walked all day and now I'm *tired*.
life /laɪf/ (n) Her *life* is difficult. She hasn't got much money.
feel /fiːl/ (v, past tense of **felt**) I *felt* ill yesterday but today I feel very well. I'm not ill now, and that's a good *feeling*.

'No problem!' Nelson ran down the road. He was happy. A lot of his friends didn't have any work. Their families were **poor** and they lived in small, old houses. They didn't have much good food or many new things. Life was difficult in the town. But Nelson had a job. Every day he **took** letters across the town and into the country for people. He was a quick runner and he took a lot of letters.

'Do you want a drink, Nelson? It's hot.' It was his **grandmother**'s sister, Ruthie. She was a big woman with a big smile.

'I can't stop!' Nelson ran **past** her. 'How's your leg now?'

'Good! Say hello to your grandmother,' Ruthie said to Nelson's back. She smiled and then she went into her small, dark house.

Nelson's legs were strong. He liked long runs. The **different** colours of houses, people and cars danced past him in a film. Sometimes pictures came into his head. They were pictures of green gardens and beautiful houses. In the pictures children played in the roads. They were happy and there were shoes on their feet. There was music in Nelson's head too – the music of his country, and always the music of his feet on the road. One, two, one, two ...

poor /pʊəʳ/ (adj) My father was *poor* but now he's got a lot of money.
took /tʊk/ (v, past tense of **take**) I *took* my books from my bag and did my homework.
grandmother /ˈgrænmʌðəʳ/ (n) One of my *grandmothers* is dead. *Granny* is my father's mother.
past /pɑːst/ (prep) Dan ran *past* the shop. Then he *passed* Mrs Brown and her daughter. In the *past*, I was a teacher. Now I'm a taxi driver.
different /ˈdɪfrənt/ (adj) My friend and I like *different* things on television. She watches football but I watch films.

Nelson was near River Street. Suddenly there was a lot of noise. It was a football game.

'Quick, Abra, you're very slow! Get the ball, now!' the **trainer shouted**. There was a tall white man with him in an expensive coat. They watched the game. The boys ran up and down with the ball. The white man talked to the trainer. Then Nelson ran past them. The boys stopped playing.

'Go, Nelson!' his friend Abra shouted. Nelson didn't look at the boys but there was a light in his eyes. He ran quickly.

The white man stopped talking to the trainer. His eyes were on Nelson. This boy was quick! Slowly he smiled.

trainer /ˈtreɪnəʳ/ (n) Tom was a very good football *trainer*. He *trained* the boys every Saturday morning. The boys *trained* from nine o'clock to one o'clock.
shout /ʃaʊt/ (v/n) Don't *shout!* I can hear you.

CHAPTER 2

'Do you like running?'

Nelson remembered the man. He was at the football game.
What did he want? Why was he in their house?

It was early in the morning. Nelson was in his small bed on the floor. The sun was on his face but his eyes were closed. In his sleep he was in a different place. He ran past a lot of people. They shouted at him, 'Go, Nelson! Go!' He smiled.

Suddenly he felt his grandmother's hand on his hand. He opened his eyes.

'Nelson! Quickly! We have a visitor.' Granny Sarah was a little old woman with a tired face but her eyes were always happy. This morning they were very big. 'It's an important man. Have you got any problems? Why is he here, Nelson?'

Nelson looked at her. 'I don't know, Granny.'

'I know, Nelson. You make me very **proud**. Your mother …'

Nelson's father and mother were dead. Granny Sarah was his family now and he loved her very much. He took his grandmother's hand. 'Let's see this important man,' he said.

The man looked very big in the small room. 'My name's Ken Banks,' he said. Nelson remembered the man. He was at the football game. What did he want? Why was he in their house?

proud /praʊd/ (adj) Helen's son is a doctor. She's very *proud* of him. 'He's a good son too,' she says *proudly*.

'Nelson.' Ken smiled and his blue eyes smiled too. 'You are a good runner.'

Nelson looked at the floor. 'Thank you, Mister.'

'Do you like running?'

Nelson looked up. 'I love it. It's my life.'

The man's eyes didn't move from Nelson's face. 'I talked to the trainer. He watches you. You run many kilometres every day. You're quick.'

'Yes,' Nelson said proudly. 'I am.'

'Listen, Nelson.' The man's face was very near Nelson's now. 'This is an important question. You can be a very good runner. You can **win races**. Do you want to do that – in here?' His hand was on Nelson's **heart**.

Nelson felt a hot light there. 'Oh yes – yes, I do.'

The man was quiet. Then he looked at Granny Sarah. 'Can he come away with me? I want to train him.'

Nelson went cold. Go away from his Granny, his life, his friends? But his grandmother's eyes were proud and happy.

'Yes,' she said quietly. 'Nelson can go with you. He can win races.'

win /wɪn/ (v, past: **won**) The Williams sisters often *win* at Wimbledon. In the years 2000–2009, Venus Williams *won* five times.
race /reɪs/ (n/v) It was a long *race* but Zoe wasn't tired.
heart /hɑːt/ (n) His *heart* stopped. Suddenly he was dead.

2.1 Were you right?

Look at your answers to Activity 1.2 on page ii. Then circle the right answers here.

1	Nelson lives with his mother.	Yes	No
2	His family is poor.	Yes	No
3	He runs every day.	Yes	No
4	He makes money from running.	Yes	No
5	Ken is a runner too.	Yes	No
6	He wants to train Nelson.	Yes	No

2.2 What more did you learn?

1 Write the names under the pictures.

Nelson Ruthie
Sarah Ken
Jacob

A 
....

B 
....

C 
....

D 
....

E 
....

2 Who says ...? Write the letters A–E.

a 'You can win races.' .....

b 'I love it. It's my life.' .....

c 'Do you want a drink?' .....

d 'He can go with you.' .....

e 'You're a good boy.' .....

2.3 Language in use

Look at the sentences on the right. Then circle the right words in these sentences.

He ran **quickly**.

He was a **quick** runner.

1 Sarah smiled *proud / proudly* at Nelson.

2 She was *proud / proudly* of him.

3 Nelson had *strong / strongly* legs.

4 His legs were *strong / strongly.*

5 He was a *good / well* runner.

6 He ran very *good / well.*

7 Sarah was a *slow / slowly* walker.

8 She walked *slow / slowly.*

9 She talked *quiet / quietly* to Ken.

10 Her words were *quiet /quietly.*

2.4 What happens next?

Are these sentences right (✓) or wrong (✗)?

1 ☐ Nelson goes to a big town.

2 ☐ He trains every day.

3 ☐ He has a room in Ken's house.

4 ☐ Ken is a bad man.

5 ☐ Nelson often visits Sarah.

6 ☐ He wins a lot of races.

7 ☐ He is proud of his family.

8 ☐ He often remembers his old friends.

CHAPTER 3

'It's in his heart.'

'You were that boy,' Marcus said quietly.
Ken's eyes went dark. 'Yes,' he said. 'I remember.'

Ken Banks took Nelson to his new home. It was Nelson's first visit to a big, new town. He felt very small in front of the tall buildings. It was a very different life here. There were shops with different things in them and many, many people. There was a lot of money in this place. And all day and all night there was noise here! Cars, people, music … The noise was always in Nelson's head.

Nelson's home now was in a big building with a lot of boys and girls. They were all runners. Every day he ran – from morning to evening. Sometimes he ran in the town on the roads. He liked that. He looked at the people and buildings. At night he was very tired but very happy.

Ken was a good trainer. 'You're quick today, Nelson! Very good!' Ken looked at the time and smiled. 'Again!' And Nelson ran again, and again, and again …

Sometimes at night his heart felt heavy. He had new friends and a new life but he wanted to see Granny Sarah. He wanted to talk to Abra and play football with him. He wanted to run past Jacob Mutwa's house and see the colours of his old life. But after some time he stopped hearing the music in his head. There was always Ken: 'Again, Nelson! Run again!'

Ken was very happy with Nelson. The boy was quick. He learned quickly too. He trained every day and he won races.

'Nelson can win at the Olympic Games,' he said to his friend Marcus. 'I want to train him for the **marathon**.'

Marcus watched Nelson. 'He's very young.'

'Yes. He's young but he's strong. He's a winner. He wants to win … it's in his heart.'

'You were that boy,' Marcus said quietly.

Ken's eyes went dark. 'Yes,' he said. 'I remember.'

◆

'I won a very important race today, Granny.' Nelson was on the telephone. 'Now I can run in the Olympics! Can you come and watch me?'

Sarah wanted to see Nelson. The boy was always in her heart. But she wasn't well. 'I'm sorry Nelson. I'm old. I can't come. But Jacob Mutwa has a television now. We can all watch your race on television.'

Nelson was angry. It was the Olympics. It was his big race.

'Nelson! Let's go out!' one of his new friends shouted.

'I'm coming!' Nelson smiled and took his coat. He stopped thinking about Granny Sarah. He had a new family now.

marathon /ˈmærəθən/ (n) The *marathon* is 42.195 kilometres.

CHAPTER 4

'He's famous.'

Nelson was angry. 'You're wrong,' he shouted. 'My father was a doctor and my mother was a teacher. We weren't poor.'

Nelson was in front again. He felt strong. One, two, one, two … and he was there! The winner! People shouted 'Nelson! Nelson!' He loved this feeling!

Nelson ran a lot of races before the Olympic Games and he won all of them. Now he was famous. People asked him questions on television and for the newspapers. They wanted to know about his life and his family. But Nelson didn't want to be the poor boy from a poor family. That wasn't his life now.

A television man came to Nelson after a race. 'Very good, Nelson! Are you going to win the marathon at the Olympics?'

Nelson smiled. 'I'm going to try!'

'You are from a poor family, Nelson. Was that difficult for you?' the man asked.

Nelson was angry. 'You're wrong,' he shouted. 'My father was a doctor and my mother was a teacher. We weren't poor. I had a good life!'

Ken listened to Nelson and the television man. He smiled. He was happy. Nelson's old life was in the past. The new Nelson was going to be famous in every country and his life was now with Ken.

Granny Sarah watched Nelson on television. She was very unhappy.

Nelson's friends and the people from his town were angry. 'Why did he say that?' they asked. 'He doesn't want to know us now because he's famous. We aren't important. Our lives are small.'

But Nelson was Sarah's boy. 'Listen!' she said. 'He's young. He's in a different town with different people. I know my boy – I know his heart. He's going to come back to us.'

But in her room at night Sarah **cried**.

cried /kraɪd/ (v, past tense of **cry**) Marina *cried* because she was very unhappy.

3.1 Were you right?

Look again at your answers to Activity 2.4. Then finish these sentences. Write a or b.

1 Nelson is tired at night because ... ...

  a he runs every day. **b** he goes out with his friends.

2 Nelson is unhappy for a short time because ... ...

  a he isn't running very well. **b** he liked his old life.

3 Sarah can't come to the Olympic Games because ... ...

  a she's ill. **b** she hasn't got the money.

4 Nelson is angry after one race because ... ...

  a he didn't win. **b** he doesn't like the TV man's questions.

5 Sarah cries at night because ... ...

  a she wants to see Nelson. **b** Nelson said some bad things.

3.2 What more did you learn?

Talk about the pictures. What are these people thinking or saying?

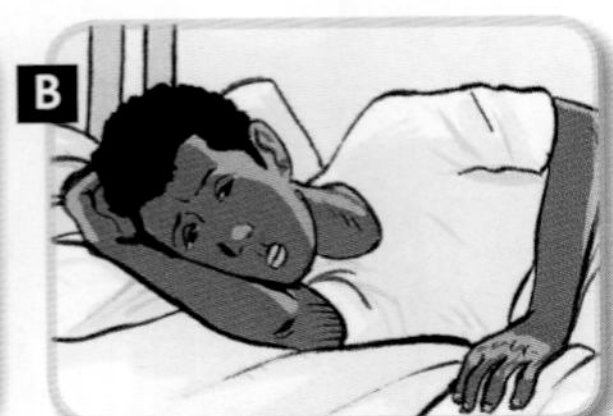

.3 Language in use

Look at the sentences on the right. Then make one sentence from these sentences, with *but*, *and* or *because*.

He had a new life **but** he wanted to see Granny Sarah.

He trained every day **and** he won races.

He doesn't want to know us now **because** he's famous.

1 Nelson can win the race. He's strong.

Nelson can win the race because he's strong.

2 Nelson got a letter from Abra. He didn't read it.

....

3 Nelson won a lot of races. Now he's famous.

....

4 Ken ran in the Olympic Games. He didn't win.

....

5 Sarah cried. She was very unhappy.

....

.4 What happens next?

Who is going to say these words? Write the names.

1 'I don't feel well.' ....

2 'Tomorrow you are going to run!' ....

3 'I'm very, very sorry.' ....

4 'We're proud of you!' ....

5 'It's going to make you strong.' ....

6 'I don't want to drink that.' ....

CHAPTER 5

'I promise.'

'I said some very bad things. I was angry. Please ...'
Nelson started to cry. He cried for his grandmother's love.

It was the day before Nelson's big Olympic race. He wanted to remember every small thing – the people, the noises, the colours.

Nelson usually ran for a long time every day. But today he only ran for a short time and then he stopped. He didn't feel well. He was hot and his head felt light. He tried to run again but there was a noise in his head. His legs weren't strong.

'Ken, I don't feel well,' he said quietly to the trainer. 'I can't run tomorrow.'

Ken looked at Nelson. The boy's face was red and hot. Yes, he was ill. But Ken's heart was in the race too. At eighteen years old, in the Olympic Games, Ken didn't finish his race. He never ran again. Now Nelson's marathon was very, very important to Ken.

'You're OK,' Ken said. 'You're tired. Go to bed this afternoon. Tomorrow is a big day. You can't be ill!'

'But Ken, I ...'

'Go to bed!' Ken's eyes were cold. 'Tomorrow you are going to run!'

Nelson went to bed. His face was hot and his hands and legs were hot too. He felt very ill. He closed his eyes and pictures danced in his head. He was a little boy again and he was ill. He was in his bed on the floor of his grandmother's house. Granny Sarah was with him. Her hand was cold on his hot head. 'You're OK, Nelson,' she said. 'Granny's here. I'm going to make you well.' She was always there. Always. He opened his eyes and looked at the telephone.

'Granny, I'm very, very sorry. I didn't phone you. I didn't write to Abra. I said some very bad things. I was angry. Please ...' Nelson started to cry. He cried for his grandmother's love.

'Ssh!' Sarah said. 'We all love you. You're a son of this town, of this country, and we're proud of you! Don't cry.'

'But – perhaps I can't win tomorrow, Granny.'

'Perhaps you can't, Nelson. But that's not important. You are going to be there – at the Olympic Games. Every child in this country is going to watch you tomorrow. They're going to think, "Nelson can be there. One day I can be there too!" **Promise** me one thing. I want to see you in the big **stadium**, in front of people from every country. Number 1, 2, 3 – that's not important. I want to see your smile on television.'

'I promise.' Nelson closed his eyes again. His head wasn't hot now and his heart felt good. But it was a big promise.

promise /ˈprɒmɪs/ (v/n) Please be home before eleven o'clock this evening. Do you *promise*?
stadium /ˈsteɪdiəm/ (n) There are 50,000 people in the football *stadium*.

CHAPTER 6

'I'm coming!'

People shouted, 'Go, Nelson!' He looked. He was near the stadium but it moved in front of his eyes

The Olympic marathon started early in the morning. Nelson was at the start with Ken. His head felt a little hot again but he didn't feel ill. Granny Sarah was good for him.

'You're going to be OK,' Ken said. 'Here, drink this.' There was a small bottle of water in his hand.

'I've got some water.' Nelson didn't understand.

Ken smiled slowly. 'This is different. It's going to make you strong.'

Nelson took the bottle and looked at it. Then he looked at Ken. 'No,' he said. 'I don't want to drink that.'

Nelson ran. His feet moved quickly on the streets of the big town. One, two, one, two … He ran past a lot of people and famous

buildings but he didn't look at them. He looked at the road and he remembered his promise. In his head was a picture of the stadium. *I'm coming! I'm coming!*

The kilometres passed and Nelson felt strong. His heart was light. He passed every runner in the race. He was happy. He liked to be in front. He listened to the music of his feet on the road. And then he looked up. There was the stadium. He looked behind him quickly. No runners! I can do this!

But suddenly his legs felt very heavy and his head was very hot again. One, two … One … two … His feet stopped. He looked at the people near him. Their mouths moved but no noise came from them. Their hands moved but they moved very slowly. The people, the buildings all danced in front of his eyes. Suddenly they weren't there. Nelson looked up. He was on the road, on his back.

One runner passed him … two runners passed him.

'Promise me.' His grandmother's face was in his head. 'I want to see your smile.'

Nelson was on his feet again. People shouted, 'Go, Nelson!' He looked. He was near the stadium but it moved in front of his eyes. Slowly he started to run again, but very, very slowly. He wanted to stop. His legs were tired and he was hot. But there was the promise. And there was the stadium.

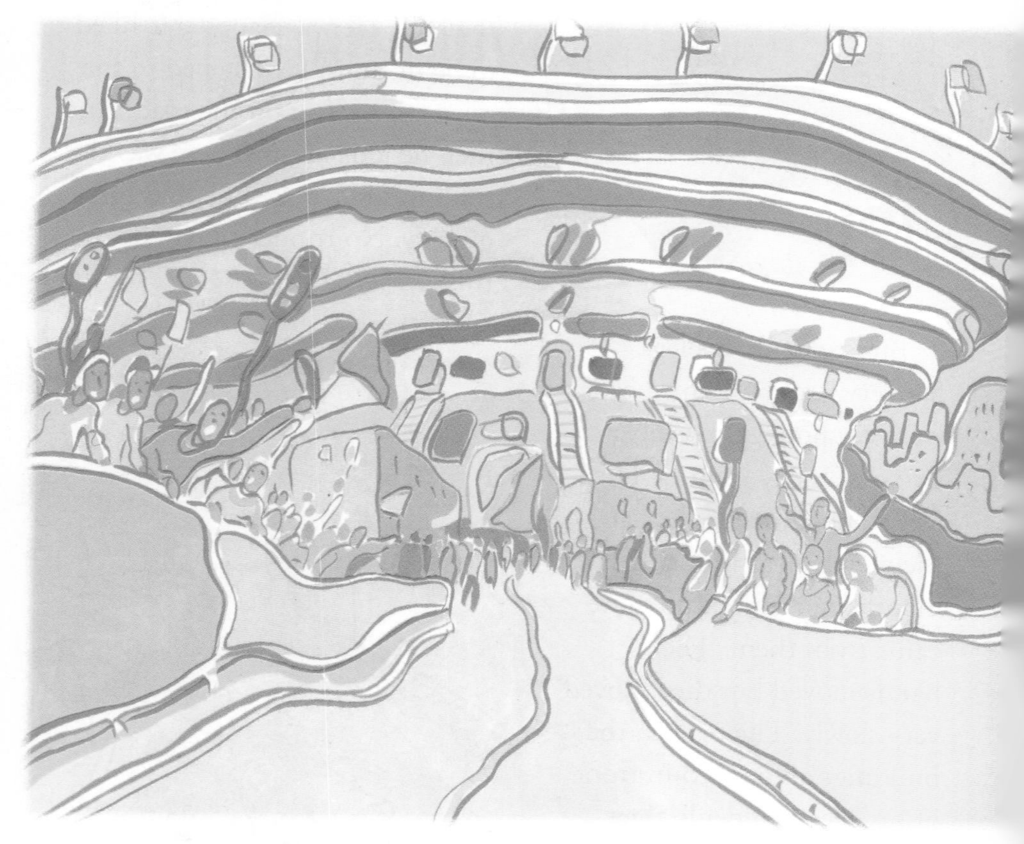

Nelson came slowly into the stadium. The noise stopped. People watched the boy. 'Can he finish?' they asked. 'Is he going to fall?'

Nelson smiled. I'm going to do this! One, two, one, two … Slowly, slowly, and then … he was there! There was a big shout. People loved him.

Nelson stopped. In front of him was the television man.

'How are you feeling, Nelson?' the man shouted. 'A lot of people are watching you! What do you want to say to them?'

But Nelson didn't want to talk. He looked at the television man and smiled, a very big smile … for his grandmother and his friends. The smile said, 'I promised, and here I am!'

Then he walked past Ken. He didn't look at his trainer and Ken looked away too. Nelson had some water and looked for a telephone. He had a lot of races in front of him, but not now. Now he wanted to go home.

Talk about it

1 Work with another student. It is a year after the Olympic Games.

Student A You are Nelson. Think about your life after the Olympic Games. Then answer the TV man's questions.

Student B You work on television. What did Nelson do after the Olympic Games? Write some questions. Then ask him.

2 Talk about these questions. What do you think?

a What bad/good things did Nelson do in the story? Why?

b What bad/good things did Ken do in the story? Why?

3 You are going to make a film about Nelson's life. Nelson is going to be in it. Talk about these questions.

a Who, from the story, do you want to be in the film with Nelson?

b What questions are you going to ask them in the film?

c What is the name of the film going to be?

Write about it

You are Nelson, Ken or Sarah. Write the page from your diary on the day of the Olympic marathon.

Today was a very important day. I ....

....

....

....

....

....

....

....

....

Nelson is a famous runner. Sometimes that is a good feeling; sometimes it isn't.

1 Talk to some friends. Do *you* want to be famous? Why (not)?

2 Work with a friend and put these words into the sentences. Are famous people happy (☺) or unhappy (☹) about these? What do you think?

friend	**remember**	**shops**	**poor**
letters	**same**	**money**	**places**
important	**newspapers**		

1	You get a lot of ...money... .	☺ .....
2	Your picture is in a lot of	.....
3	You meet .... people.	.....
4	A lot of people want to be your	.....
5	You can give money to .... people.	.....
6	You work in a lot of different	.....
7	People write .... to you.	.....
8	Young people want to do the .... things.	.....
9	Sometimes you don't .... your old friends.	
10	People know you in the	.....

3 People are famous for many different jobs.

a Write the name of a famous person under every picture of a job. Why is your person famous? Write two or three words.

b Talk to your friends about the people but don't say the names. Do your friends know these people?

He's a Spanish footballer but he plays for Liverpool.

4 Who is very, very famous today?

a Work with a friend. Choose three people and find interesting things about them on the Internet.

b Talk to a lot of different friends. Which famous people did they choose? Why? Make a list of ten very famous people.

c Write about two of the people on the list.